PRAISE FOR
THE TENSORATE SERIES

"Yang's masterful world-building is on display.... The Old World feel of their 'silkpunk' fantasy is made modern by smoothly interwoven gender-nonbinary characters, whose richness enhances the emotional impact of this short but compelling work."

—*Booklist* on *The Descent of Monsters*

"Joyously wild stuff. Highly recommended."

—**N. K. Jemisin,** *The New York Times*

"Yang conjures up a world of magic and machines, wild monsters and sophisticated civilizations, that you'll want to return to again and again."

—**Annalee Newitz,** *Ars Technica*

"Full of love and loss, confrontation and discovery. Each moment is a glistening pearl, all strung together in a wonder of world creation."

—**Ken Liu, author of** *The Grace of Kings*

"I love JY Yang's effortlessly fascinating world-building."
—**Kate Elliott, author of** *Black Wolves* **and** *Court of Fives*

"A fascinating world of battles, politics, magic, and romance."
—**Zen Cho, author of** *Sorcerer to the Crown*

"Like a Miyazaki movie decided to jump off the screen and sear itself into prose, and in doing so became something entirely new."
—**Indrapramit Das, author of** *The Devourers*

"Relentlessly captivating, heartbreaking, and powerful."
—**Fran Wilde, author of** *Updraft*

"Filled with memorable characters and set in a wonderfully imaginative and original universe."
—**Aliette de Bodard, author of**
The House of Shattered Wings

"Yang's prose carries the reader along."
—*Locus* **on** *The Black Tides of Heaven*

"Yang deftly creates a world infused with magic, story, and hierarchy."
—**Joel Cunningham,** *B&N Sci-Fi and Fantasy Blog*

"Yang captures an epic sweep in compact, precise prose."
—*Publishers Weekly* on *The Black Tides of Heaven* (starred review)

ALSO BY JY YANG

THE TENSORATE SERIES

The Black Tides of Heaven
The Red Threads of Fortune
The Descent of Monsters

JY YANG

THE ASCENT TO GODHOOD

A TOM DOHERTY ASSOCIATES BOOK

NEW YORK

This is a work of fiction. All of the characters, organizations, and events portrayed in this novella are either products of the author's imagination or are used fictitiously.

THE ASCENT TO GODHOOD

Copyright © 2019 by JY Yang

Cover illustration by Yuko Shimizu
Cover design by Christine Foltzer

Edited by Carl Engle-Laird

A Tor.com Book
Published by Tom Doherty Associates
120 Broadway
New York, NY 10271

www.tor.com

Tor® is a registered trademark of
Macmillan Publishing Group, LLC.

ISBN 978-1-250-16587-9 (ebook)
ISBN 978-1-250-16588-6 (trade paperback)

First Edition: July 2019

For you, who feels seen when you read these books

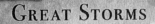

GREAT STORMS

ENDLESS SEAS

GUSAI DESERT

x.

BATANAAR

xv.

vi.

GAUR ANTAM

VISHARAN

TIGUMAN

ix.

NAM MIN

xi.

viii.

MATAPUR

ATHARAYABAD

EL ZAHARAD

THIEN CHIH

THE FIRE ISLANDS

DEMONS' OCEAN

THE QUARTERLANDS

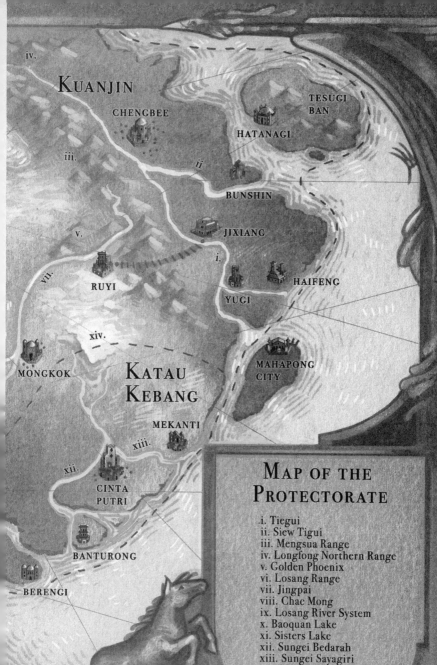

KUANJIN

CHENGBEE

TESUGI BAN

HATANAGI

BUNSHIN

JIXIANG

RUYI

HAIFENG

YUGI

MAHAPONG CITY

MONGKOK

KATAU KEBANG

MEKANTI

CINTA PUTRI

BANTURONG

BERENGI

iv.

iii.

ii

i.

v.

vii.

xiv.

xiii.

xii.

MAP OF THE PROTECTORATE

i. Tiegui
ii. Siew Tigui
iii. Mengsua Range
iv. Longfong Northern Range
v. Golden Phoenix
vi. Losang Range
vii. Jingpai
viii. Chac Mong
ix. Losang River System
x. Baoquan Lake
xi. Sisters Lake
xii. Sungei Bedarah
xiii. Sungei Sayagiri
xiv. White Plateau
xv. Kitesuaran Range

•••|||||••• = Mengsua Pass

Chapter One

What do you want? Can't a woman have a drink in peace these days? I'm not in the mood to talk. Look at all these motherfuckers partying it up, celebrating the news. Well, good for them. I'm in mourning.

See, the woman I love is dead. Funny, watching everyone cheer what you've been working for all these years, yet feeling nothing but sorrow. Go join the party and leave me alone. I've earned some time to grieve.

Alright, you're persistent. I see that. Who did you say you were again?

Well, I don't know you. And Akeha has many acquaintances I don't care for. Why should I listen to what you have to say?

Yeah, yeah, sure. Everyone's got a sob story. Look. I'm sure your lady, whoever it was, you loved her, too. Bet it hurts like hell. Bet it does. But no one knows what it's like for me. You think you do, but you really don't.

So, your lover was a Tensor. What of it? Of course I know who she was. Akeha kept me updated. Do you think the Machinists don't communicate? I'm their leader.

I don't have time for this.

Fine. If you're going to stand there and bother me, you might as well buy me a drink. At least I'll get something out of it.

You know, I'm surprised. You don't look like the kind of person who would be with a Tensor. Don't puff up; that's a compliment. Hah. But I get it. I get it. Look at my life, after all.

Tell me a bit about you. How did you come here? How did you get into this mess?

"A lowlife just like you?" If you're trying to get in my good books, you're not doing a very good job. So, you were an outlaw. Born in the margins, were you? How much of the real Tensorate did your beloved show you? You know I saw everything. I was on top of the world, at the peak of heaven.

That was a life, that it was.

It's funny. All those years ago, when I was just a girl, and *she* was just a girl . . . who could have guessed what would happen? What she would become. What I would become. It's funny.

If you want to hear the story, I can tell you. Heaven knows nobody wants to hear her side of it, and with her dead now, maybe nobody ever will. No one can tell her story like I can. There was no one else as close to her, you know? No one . . .

Strange days upon us. Her guiding hand is gone. The Protectorate is about to change in ways none of us can predict. We're plunging toward an unknown future. And I . . . I am an old woman. The time for me to weave and play with the threads of fortune is long over.

Hekate's gone. Maybe once I tell this story, I'll be able to release her from this hollow inside me, where she's been trapped for so long.

Take a seat. Get comfortable. Get yourself a drink. Take notes, if you want. This is a story few have the privilege of knowing.

Chapter Two

Where do I even start? Where do you begin a tale that tangles like a bramble across the years and twines with the fine and cruel threads of fortune? How do I tell the story of the one who burned the world to ash around her and rebuilt it in her image, when it's the same story as my greatest and deepest heartbreak? How do I balance the silhouette of my private emotions with the vast scale of the world turning around me?

Maybe I'll start from the beginning. My beginning. After all, I'm the one telling the story, am I not?

I was born in a small village north of Jixiang, the third of seven children. My parents were farmers. Most everybody was. It was a poor area and we were poor people. Growing vegetables was the only way to get by. Nostalgia puts a taste in your mouth, doesn't it? When I think back on those days, I remember peace. The mountains at dawn, draped in white mist, the smell of fresh-cut grass, the feel of loamy clay between my toes. Mother kept an enormous pot of congee bubbling on the stove. Its fragrance greeted you when you walked through the door.

Ah, the crisp scent of shallots frying! Sometimes, I think I miss it more than anything else: that smell, in that kitchen, combined with the waft of the jasmine growing in the front courtyard.

What about you? You look Kebangilan. Grew up on the coast, did you? Different climate, different foods . . . but poverty tastes the same everywhere. Boiled food, everything watery, too cold or too hot. The dreams I had in those days! All I wanted was to escape the grey, rocky life that I led. I imagined simple pleasures: a house with stone walls, a little garden, a goat or two . . . My imagination was so small back then. So pure.

The year I turned twelve was a hard one. The rains came too much in the winter, and then not at all. Crops grew spindly and yellow in our fields, fish died in the ponds, and a pallor of death wafted through the air in the heated evenings. It was a strange year to come into adulthood. The world was withering and blackening around me, yet there I was, hips and thighs growing plump, legs and arms growing long and strong like tree branches. One morning, I put on my trousers and realized how high their hems hung above my ankles. When had that happened? I couldn't say. Changes. They just sneak up on you, the little bastards.

That was the first thing I learned that summer. The second was that there is no logic to the world. No balance.

The world outside my window was dying, yet my body was flourishing. Where was all that energy, that life coming from?

The dust and brittleness of my village were disturbed by a new arrival just as the last of my mother's rice ran out. A man—no, a vulture. A scavenger waiting for the moment before a living thing became fresh meat. We were a family of eight crammed into that small wooden shack with one stove: five children, my parents, one remaining grandmother. I remember staring up at that man as he stood in the doorway with his smooth face and his neat robe in deep colors, and the idiot child that I was thought he was the most handsome thing I'd ever seen. How important he looked! His gaze swept over me and my siblings huddled listlessly in the heat, and my heart stopped when his eyes settled on me.

What did he see in me? That I was pretty? That people would pay money for my company? That I was this poor and gullible little fuck with shiny round eyes?

Maybe he wasn't even thinking that far. Maybe he was just plucking up children like peaches off a tree.

You have to understand, out in those areas, we didn't do gender like they did in the capital. You get born as one thing, you're expected to stick to it. I popped out, they looked at me, said *girl,* and that's how it was. Do I have regrets about it? No, but I'm sure there are many who do. But when things are that hard, and food is a struggle every season, people cling to structure. It makes life easier, see? So, my parents wouldn't part with sons, my sister was too old, and the youngest was just a baby. Worthless, just another mouth to feed. Couldn't put it to work, could we? So, what was left? Just little me.

I don't know if my parents ever regretted selling me to put food in my siblings' mouths. They were typical farmer stock, not the kind to talk about their feelings, or very much at all. Only my older sister, Xiuqing, cried when she heard. I don't know if I cried in return. She had one precious thing, a carved jade elephant she'd been given by a passing merchant. She pressed it into my hands. *Come back soon,* she said, clinging to dull hope that my going away was only temporary. *Remember us,* she said. I told her it was impossible I would ever forget her. Then I was whisked away from the only place I had ever known.

On nights I can't sleep, I like to torment myself with an imagined world where my sister was taken instead of me. A world where my big sister became a courtesan and I stayed behind in her place. What would I be? A seam-stress? A farmer? Some dull lad's wife with swollen ankles and a voice hoarse from shouting? I'd have a swarm of children, too. Children to look after the house, children to tend to the fields . . . Children! Fuck, I'd be miserable. No, I don't regret my life at all. So, I fucked up in all directions, but at least it was an exciting fuckup, you know?

Of course, I know that's not true. Even my sister did not end her life as a simple farmer. Maybe I would have become a rebel all the same. Maybe it's in my family's blood, all this getting into trouble.

Right. I get distracted. So many memories. It's been such a long time since I've thought of my girlhood, it's easy to get lost in nostalgia. Lost in myself.

You know, all those years, she never asked me about my past. She didn't think it was relevant. Never did. And you know, I felt the same. I threw away my whole life for her. My whole identity. I wanted to.

Anyway. There I was, twelve years old, never been farther than two days' trek from my village, being brought to the capital. The man who bought me was called Wei. I don't know if it was his real name. I never found out, and I was never able to track him down afterward. He was nice to me, at first. Made sure I ate enough, made sure I slept enough, had a bag of soft, floured sweets that he would offer me during our long journey. He presented me with marvel after marvel. I'd never been in that kind of cart. I'd never seen slackcraft, ever. I would stick my head out to watch the ground speeding by under us as we floated over it.

Wei bought three other girls during his trip: two who were already traveling with him, and one he picked up in the village next to mine. Their names . . . let's see, what were they? There was Yixing, of course. And I think the other two were Sara and Min. He told them my name was Huarong, which it was not, but because he said so, that's what it became. Why the surprised face? You think I was born Lady Han? No. That too was someone else's name for me.

All of us were about the same age, except for Sara, who was older, maybe sixteen years old. Tanned and broad from working in the fields, like a boy. Min was very quiet. Then there was Yixing, my neighbor-girl, who I had an automatic connection with. I don't think we became friends, but it felt like that. I had no one else to talk to.

Ah, Chengbee! The city of the golden phoenix, the cradle of the Protectorate! You're a provincial, like me, so you must remember what it felt like to encounter the capital for the first time. The red peaked roofs, shoulder to shoulder, stretching all the way to the foot of the mountains. The throngs in the markets, shoulder to shoulder, filling the air with the noise of their bargaining. The dense smells that come and go as you pass along the street: chestnuts in hot sand, the steam off soup cauldrons, the sewage in the back alleys. Wei took the cart into the densest parts of the city, and the whole way, I peeked out of the window with my mouth hanging open. How could I not? My senses were being assaulted from every direction, on every level. I had never imagined that people could live like this, stacked on top of one another, in constant motion and contact. The city felt so alive, but in a different way from the mountains and fields that I knew. Out in the countryside, being among living things feels full and serene. Everything in Chengbee is small and frantic.

Our cart passed through the hot, bright center of the city and kept going. I thought we might stop at one of the many inns with their silk ribbons and gilded signs, but we didn't. Slowly, the buildings grew sparser, the people on the street fewer and more poorly dressed. I asked Wei, *Where are we going?* I still trusted him at that point. I thought he would take care of us. But he just said, *Don't worry your silly head about it*, and barely looked at me.

We stopped at a training school, although I didn't know what it was then. The school was five or six buildings connected by courtyards, and it had clearly seen better times, maybe as an administrative center or one of those specialized Tensor academies. By the time we got there, its glory days were long over. Tiles sagged on the roof, and the dedication to the Protectorate, painted in gold, had faded to the color of dirt.

A woman named Madam Wong met us at the door;

she was in charge of the place. Wei had us all get out of the cart and stand in a row, while Madam Wong examined us in turn, looking at our faces and teeth, making us turn around. Like horses on sale. Asking us questions to check our diction and bearing. *Can you sing? Have you danced before?* She asked me what my name was; I said *Huarong.* If I was going to live in Wei's world, I might as well use the name that he gave me.

Out of the lineup, Madam Wong chose Yixing and me. She had no use for the other two. In we went, and out went Wei with the heavy little pouch she gave him. He didn't turn back. Didn't offer any parting words to the two girls whose lives he just threw down a completely different path. Just another working day for him.

As for Min and Sara, who knows what happened to them? Wei probably sold Sara off as a laborer: strong girl like her, and brown too. You know how these people operate—of course you do. Of course you do. I don't know about Min. Possibly she was auctioned off too. She didn't talk much—or maybe she couldn't—but she wasn't stupid, and she seemed hardworking. There was one time much later, when I was living in the Great High Palace, that I thought I saw her. One of the local magistrates who came to speak with Hekate had a servant girl about the right size and age. She had the same kind of energy, too, that same limpid silence. A big patch of scarring down one cheek. I couldn't say if it was Min. It had been so long since I'd seen her, and the years in between had erased the lines of my memories enough that any hundred generic faces could have stood in for that pale girl I barely knew. I like to think she survived. I like to think that she still lives on, somewhere in this hope-forsaken land.

But Min's not relevant to the story.

Madam Wong began training Yixing and me at once. You know what's going on, don't you? I'd been sold as an entertainer girl. One of the fancy ones who look pretty and smile at parties to make elites feel like their position in society has some benefits. I had to learn to dance, I had to learn to play the zither, I had to learn the hundred and forty stanzas of romantic poetry. I, an almost-illiterate peasant girl, had to pick up things that noble children are taught from birth in six months so I could make some whiskery old administrator feel good about himself while he leered at me. Luckily for me, I learn fast. I had no natural talent for any of it—Madam Wong said I danced like I wanted to strangle somebody—but I was good enough to pass.

Poor Yixing wasn't. She was a simple girl, goodhearted, but she had clumsy fingers and a bad memory. Day after day, she would try to grasp the basics of music and dancing and the Chengbee accent, and day after day, she would be sent to bed with her ears and face stinging red from Madam Wong's slaps. She would be forced to skip meals until she got this and that right. *Good for nothing!* Madam Wong used to say. *Filthy peasant! You wouldn't be hungry if you weren't so lazy.*

Yixing would come to me and beg me for help, but what could I do? She wasn't cut out for that kind of life. *Just work harder,* I would tell her. *You don't have to be good, just okay. Either that, or you can run away.*

But she never did. I woke up one morning to find her hanging from the wooden beams of the roof, her body already stiff and cold. She'd used one of the silk scarves we'd been learning to dance with. She saw no other way out.

You know what Madam Wong said? *What a waste.* A waste of her time and her money! She was pissed that she didn't get what she paid Wei for. Probably complained to him about it.

Should I have done more for her? What could I have done? At that time, I was focused on one thing and one thing only: my own survival. You think that makes me selfish? I never said I was perfect. Who among us is?

Chapter Three

I graduated from the training school much faster than the other girls—most took three or four years of training, but I was gone in two. Maybe it was Yixing's death that motivated me, or maybe I just wanted to escape Madam Wong and those musty rooms. I wanted more out of my life. With this fire in me, I spent every waking moment perfecting my gait, my speech, my way of thinking. I had to act like a highborn girl and master the low arts.

I hate that name, you should know. *Low?* There's nothing low about it. Providing pleasure on demand is as much a skill as any other art form. It takes as much finesse as playing the zither. As much cunning as negotiating a peace treaty. People who mock dancing girls would fail if they tried to do our jobs. Judgmental worms. What do they know?

I was sent to a dancing house to join other girls Madam Wong had trained. Of course, a girl of my caliber would never end up serving in a common inn—as if the upper crust would go to one of those places to rub shoulders and share cups with lowly merchants and artisans.

They held their parties in their houses, with dancing girls delivered by order. In the morning, a trusted servant would come over and we'd line up like goats in a marketplace. The servants chose girls they knew their masters would like, and we would have the rest of the day to get ready.

I was fourteen, nearly fifteen. We weren't allowed to go alone with the men until we were sixteen—not because the house cared about our welfare, mind, but because some shit went down in the past with the younger girls and left a huge mess to clean up. So, the houses were just covering their asses. My first year, I danced and poured wine and smiled at old men, but that was all. I watched and learned from the other girls, the ones who were doing the work. It was . . . informative.

I also met Tensors for the first time. All my training did nothing to help me deal with them. A clear-minded Tensor could throw you across the room without lifting a finger, or crush you into the ground, or shock you with electricity. Like *this*. Ha! Look at you jump. It took me *months* before I could go near one without shaking. Ironic, you know? If you think about what I became.

When I came of age, my first offering was snapped up by a Tensor named Chong. A short, bulky man with a mean sense of humor, he took himself extremely seriously. He had been eyeing me for some time. He was, at that time, assistant to the Minister of Agriculture, and in the noble houses we danced in, it was whispered that he was next in line for that post. Yes, I know you've never heard of him. Don't jump ahead. You'll find out why later. Chong was busy ass-patting the senior administration, so he threw extravagant parties every two weeks, and I became a fixture at those parties. He liked me. He liked me a lot. And he knew I was ripening, so he pressured Madam Wong to let him have the first bite. I was coveted in those days. A real prize. But how could Madam Wong say no to him? He was going to be *Minister*.

Chong wasn't gentle, but it could have been worse. The stories I've heard: I knew I got lucky. Chong was ugly and clumsy and selfish in bed, but he was easy to please. Easy to manipulate. He liked me, and he thought I liked him, too. I became a regular in his bedchambers. Probably more than his wife. Small, quiet woman. I pitied her. Imagine spending most of your life trapped in the gilded cage of a mansion, only free to do whatever pleased a man like Chong. As though the fortunes gave everyone else a plate of rice and she got a bucket of shit instead.

I told myself, *I am not going to be like that. I will find a way to become someone who can do as she likes.*

And then the fortunes brought me to her, and my life was set upon a path I could never have imagined.

I see that look in your eye. I know what you're thinking: it was love at first sight, me instantly ensnared by the webs of fortune. What a *romantic* idea. But reality is nothing like that.

Imagine. I was a courtesan, a dancing girl, and she a guest—the middle child of the Protector, a girl fated to be married off to some sniveling bureaucrat as a reward for his good behavior. But still. She was nobility, and I was nothing. The first time she saw me, it was at one of Chong's parties. As his influence grew, so did his appetite for wine and women. There were parties every week, sometimes twice a week. Everyone who wanted to be someone tried to attend them. Tedious as hell, but it gave me the opportunity to charm the upper crust. I was sitting in Chong's lap, laughing at one of his mediocre jokes, and there was this girl, staring from across the room. I don't know why I caught her eye, or why she caught mine. She was so focused. All this music and song and dance around her, yet she was fixated on me. Bloody creepy.

Later, I found out who she was, and that made it worse. Why would the Protector's daughter be interested in me? She led a life in the heavens, and I was a bug in the dirt. Her wordless attention was unsettling.

Hekate didn't show up at the next party, or the one after that. Every time, I looked specifically for her, and every time, I was glad my search failed. I began to relax. I was happy for our interaction to remain nothing more than one night of acute discomfort on my part. Even as the party favorite of a rising star, I knew that the Protector's family lived in a world beyond mine. A momentary brush with their like was all I needed and wanted. No more.

A month after our first meeting, there was a grand party in the Great High Palace itself. The Protector's youngest had just had his gender confirmed, which called for a huge and extravagant celebration. Everyone who was anyone was invited, and naturally they needed entertainers. Of *course*. Couldn't lay that burden on the Protector's concubines, could they? Palace staff sent for girls from all around the Protectorate. Madam Wong picked a contingent of six from her menagerie as an offering of congratulations. This included me, of course. By now, my status was quite unrivaled within her ranks of girls.

All of us were terrified, but more than that, we were *excited*. The Great High Palace—imagine! None of us had been inside, or even near the grounds. We had only heard stories of its size and opulence. That you had to take a cart to get from one end to the other. That its gardens were bigger than any mansion and had trees that grew nowhere else in the Protectorate, or on Ea, for that matter. We thought the fruit of those trees could grant you immortality, or the power of flight, or the ability to shapeshift. We whispered about ponds the width of lakes, in whose depths swam gold and silver fish as big as horses. The rafters and nooks of the house rippled with our wild tales.

Of course, I knew that *she* would be there, that strange daughter, but I gave it no thought. Of course she wouldn't remember me. Why would she? I was a dancing girl she'd seen only once, many months ago. I would be busy, she would have her filial duties to attend to. Nothing was going to happen.

On the day of the party, a cart came for us several hours before the festivities started. The six of us were primed, powdered, scented, and decorated. Everything had to be ready early, all warmed up when the guests arrived.

Was the Great High Palace anything like I'd expected? Yes and no. How do you compare a dream and reality? They don't exist in the same world and don't follow the same rules. The palace seemed as large as a country to me, with an uncountable number of rooms and corridors and courtyards. Was it as magical as it had been in the stories we shared with one another? Of course not. But it was more intimidating because it was real. We all felt awe, terror. If you'd been inside, you would too.

The party was held in the main receiving hall and

spilled out to neighboring buildings. The main hall could only seat seventy for a banquet, after all. The two hundred dancing girls were split into eight groups and rotated amongst the buildings so that the attendees got a sample of all of us. No, we weren't expected to service them all—are you nuts? None of that was going to happen under *that* Protector's nose. You weren't born yet, were you? You're too young. So, the only Protector you've known is Hekate. Well. Her father was *famously* prudish. He didn't even make use of his concubines; they were just for show. Tradition and all. His son and close associates kept them busy. We were really only there to dance. Everything to be kept above the navel, you know?

I first caught a glimpse of her in the main hall, by the front but not at the same table as the Protector. Our eyes met like this—and my heart jumped in my chest—but her attention immediately turned somewhere else. I thought, *She doesn't remember me. Good.*

There were so many people in that hall, greatest of all the Protector himself. I'd seen light captures of him, of course, but in person he seemed so much . . . smaller. For the first time, it struck me that he was just another human being. An imperfect man, with bad teeth and sagging folds of skin. A man who turned red with wine, just like anybody else. Who choked on food when laughing, just like anybody else.

He was *mortal,* just like any of us.

After an hour, my group was sent to the next hall to sing and dance and smile our fake smiles. That was that for my interaction with the Protector's daughter, I thought. Maybe I was disappointed. I think I was mostly relieved.

Halfway through the night, a royal servant came and tapped me on the shoulder. From her makeup I knew she was somebody's handmaid. She said, *Follow me.* Was I in trouble? What did she want? I was worried, but I followed her anyway. As the lowest of the low, all I could do was follow orders. My life was nothing. My wants were nothing.

It was already dark, and I was nervous. The loose sunballs floating between the rafters cast pools of shadow upon the ground. Within them I imagined all kinds of assassins or thieves or similar bastards lying in wait. I wasn't supposed to be there. I wasn't supposed to leave the main celebrations. I could only imagine the terrible fates that would befall me.

Still, I forged on. I was curious to see what would happen, you see.

We stopped at a garden square. In its middle was a neat pavilion in which a small figure stood, unmoving and straight-backed.

She's waiting for you, the girl said.

I went obediently to the pavilion. Even before the figure turned around, I knew exactly who she was. Still, I was completely unprepared for her. My heart stopped in my chest when I saw her face. I felt something precious break in me. You know how it feels—in here.

She said, *You're Chong's pet.*

It was the first time I'd heard her speak. And her voice—it was nothing like I'd expected. It was so . . . soft. And it had a texture to it, like paper.

I was so surprised, I said nothing in return. She reacted like I was an idiot: Are *you Chong's pet? I'm talking to you.*

I snapped back: *What the hell do you want?* See, I get rude when I'm poked. In the dancing house, they sometimes called me Spiny Badger.

Luckily for me, she wasn't offended. In fact, she laughed. She was so used to people bowing and scraping for her, my vulgarity was refreshing. She said, *So, this is the kind of woman Chong likes? I was right; sniveling weasels like him always want to be bullied in bed.*

I told her, *You still haven't answered my question.*

She laughed again and took my hand, like this. I was shocked and pulled away. My anger had shielded me from how much danger I was in, but that point of contact brought it all back. She could kill me without consequence. Or do worse. So what if she had no political power—she was the Protector's daughter and I was just a dancing girl. A dancing girl who should have been at the party and not wandering the tangled guts of the Palace. If she said she caught me trying to steal the Protector's treasures, who would they believe?

But she didn't look angry. Her thoughts were hard to read even back then. That cheebyekia was a master at showing exactly what she wanted people to see. And I didn't know that yet.

She said, *I need your help.*

I said, *For what? What could you possibly want from a dancing girl like me?*

She said, *You know Chong, don't you? You're the only one who spends time inside his bedchambers.*

I knew right away she wanted me to do something dangerous. Which was scary. But it was also exciting. I was still young. I viewed every unexpected circumstance as a chance to change my life.

I said, *Don't tell me you want me to kill him.*

She laughed again. And back then, when she was a young woman, she had a beautiful laugh. It was like . . . I don't know, like light reflecting off a lake. Whatever, I'm not a poet.

She told me, *I want you to steal his private records. His letters, his business ledgers. I want you to bring them to me.*

Why? I asked.

And she said, *Because I want to get rid of him, why else?*

Immediately, I was suspicious. I was young, I was

naive, but I was not an idiot. She didn't know me. She didn't know what I thought. How did she know I wouldn't spill everything to Chong instead?

I asked, *Why do you think I'll do it?*

And she said, *You steal from him, don't you?*

You see, I'd been taking things from clients' rooms. Small things, things I thought they wouldn't miss. The bastards were all so rich, who would notice a bauble or two missing? A few of the girls and I had a network inside the dancing house. After we had satisfied our clients, we put a few drops of sleeping draught in their sweet wine and then hid small trinkets in specially designed pouches in our clothes. The trinkets were worth a lot on the black market, and we had a contact who fenced them for us.

You see, us dancing girls, we weren't paid. The house provided us with food and clothes and shelter; what more could we want? We knew that if we wanted to escape that life, and make choices of our own, we needed money.

But I was careless, and maybe a bit greedy. If I had taken only one or two things, Chong wouldn't have noticed. But every time I went to his place, I made sure to steal something. Stupid, right? After months of this, Chong realized that many of his small statues and penholders and other jeweled things were missing, and I became the main suspect. He had talked to some Tensors about setting traps to catch me with my ass unwashed. He talked loud enough that Hekate had caught wind of it.

So, she said, *We have a common enemy. I can help you, and you can help me.*

Why do you want to blackmail Chong? I asked.

And she said, *I don't want to blackmail him. I want to destroy him.*

I figured out the reason later, by piecing together hints I gathered. How much do you know about the Protectorate's line of succession? Surely, something that important would reach you even on the renegade seas? No?

Alright, look. It's like this. The Protector is succeeded by the first child of the next generation of royals. That means the children of the current Protector, and the children of all their siblings. The pool can get quite large. Hekate's father was actually second in line—he had an older sister who was Protector before him, but she died young, some kind of sickness, and he ascended to the Celestial Throne. He was due to be succeeded by the oldest of the next generation.

That was Sanao Kamine, the first and only child of the Protector's sister, the one who died. Hekate's oldest cousin. She didn't like him; she thought her older brother, born a few years after Kamine, would be a better, fairer ruler. And it was true: Kamine was a shitbucket. He wasn't just corrupt and petty; he was also lazy and vain. He would have driven the Protectorate into the ground.

It's probably hard for someone your age to imagine, but in those days, the Protectorate was struggling to hold itself together. There was unrest in the south, where the Kebangilan royalty were quietly stoking rebellious sentiment. The Protectorate needed a strong leader if it was to thrive, and that little bastard was not it.

Now, at that time, Chong was on Kamine's side in the war of succession. So, naturally, he and Hekate were enemies. But she never said any of this to me. She was too clever for that. She let me think she was carrying out some petty vendetta against Chong, because highborns have nothing better to do.

I said, *What do I gain from this?* I was on the hind foot in this exchange, but as a young fool, I was always testing my luck.

And would you know it, my luck held. Because she just laughed. And then she kissed me.

I never expected that. The gulf between who she was and who I was—it just wasn't appropriate. I was too startled to reciprocate. Before I regained my balance, she pressed a small, lacquered box into my hand. Inside were two things: one a primitive beacon, a little button like this. Back in those days, you just pressed it and it sent an alert to the other side. Nothing like the fancy talkers you have nowadays. The other thing was a pretty carved ball of jade with something shimmering and metal knotted in the middle.

I knew what the beacon was, but the second item confused me. *What is this?* I asked.

She said, *This will break slackcraft wards in any room you leave it in. Hide it in Chong's room, and you won't get caught stealing. In return, bring me what I want.*

My mind reverted to practicalities because it couldn't process anything else. I asked the only thing I could think of: *How?*

She said, *Use the beacon. I will send for you.* And she smiled.

Chapter Four

I knew that I had been tipped into madness, thrown into an arena where dragons fought, where a mere mortal like me did not belong. But I was young. I was scared, and excited, and I was also a fool. I wanted to the play the dragons' game. I wanted to play *her* game. I was flattered that she'd picked me. That's the problem with being vain. In the days that followed, I kept replaying the kiss in my mind. The memory of her lips was a ghost haunting me. I couldn't stop thinking about *her*.

A week after the party, Chong called me to his bedchambers. I boldly wore Hekate's gift around my waist like a bauble. Back then, I had more bravery than sense in my head. Plus, I knew my way around Chong, you know? I figured I knew how to distract him.

He strung me right along. Chong was a crafty man, after all. Since he was charmless and not particularly gifted, his only weapons were cunning and ass-kissing. He let me think everything was normal. We got into the rhythm of things, all the touching and giggling. He slipped a hand to my waist, like he was going to undo my sash, but he touched the little box. *What is this?* he asked, all fake-innocent. I knew at that moment that I'd been found out.

He tried to grab my hands to restrain me. And that's where he made his mistake. All our time together, I had been pliant toward him, giving in to his demands or only putting up a token struggle. Like, *Oh no, please don't, you're so bad, darling.* Giggle. He thought he was stronger than me. But he wasn't. I grew up working the paddies. And even if we learned calligraphy and the daintiest ways of pouring tea in the dancing house, we still had to carry water and scrub the floors. The only difference is that we did it with gloves on. To protect our hands, see?

I clocked him in the head. He went down so fast, I thought I'd killed him. Thankfully, the bastard was still breathing when I checked.

I was panicking. I couldn't explain my way out of this. When Chong woke up, the game would be over. I would be arrested, Hekate would be implicated, that would be the end. My life as a spy destroyed before it even began.

I thought briefly of killing him. I could make it look like an accident! Maybe I could get away with it! He wouldn't be around to tell people otherwise!

But I couldn't. I wasn't far enough gone to be a murderer yet. The thought of taking a life filled me with a shudder of fear. Death was such a terrible, irreversible solution. Plus, my gut said it would only get me in more trouble. I dragged Chong onto the bed and decided to continue as though he was just asleep. I had to give my best effort. If I met an ugly fate, at least I would do so knowing I had shaped my own destiny.

I had to find a place to hide Hekate's device. Of course I was going to leave it in the room. I had no doubt that Chong would eventually find it and its presence would implicate Hekate. Already, I was thinking it would be good for me if her fate was tied to mine. I started prying at the floorboards, seeing if any of them would come loose.

One did. Lifting it up revealed several bundles of red silk, some pale and ragged with age. I unwrapped one and found scrolls and record sticks inside. As though guided by invisible threads of fate, I had found exactly what I was looking for.

I had to work fast. Chong might wake any moment. I shoved Hekate's device into the nook, and bundled everything into my robes and snuck out. I was lucky not to be stopped, because there were at least a dozen packages, and I did a shit job of hiding them under my bosom. Our cart-driver was very good, sworn to secrecy—he knew what was going on, but he never sold out any of us girls. Once I was in the cart, I activated the beacon. My heart was wild in my chest, and my mind was wild with fear and excitement. I had done the unthinkable. I had no idea what would happen next.

Hekate worked fast. By the time we got back to the dancing house, one of her handmaidens was waiting outside with the royal cart. Waiting for me, of course. I didn't even get the chance to go back inside, change my clothes, wash my face, anything. Just straight on to the Great High Palace.

Upon arrival, the girl took me and all my loot straight to Hekate's bedchambers. Not a person along the corridors bothered us. After all, I was being escorted by someone serving the Protector's immediate family. And even though I was afraid of all the things that could go wrong, I felt comforted knowing I had the protection of the highest powers in the land. It felt so calming. Invulnerability, you know? It was so alien to me, the girl who had been nothing before she became a commodity. And it was so good.

I still remember what she wore when I saw her waiting for me. It was a yellow gown of the fanciest silk, paperthin and so fine you could see right through it. So fragile you couldn't embroider it, so the butterfly motif had to be painted on. Her hair was loose around her shoulders and her face barely painted. I was startled to see her like that, almost naked in that room, the most intimate setting of her gilded life. I thought we were there to conduct business of a different kind. When I drew close, I smelled that she had also anointed her skin with perfumed oils. Her favorite kind of jasmine, the particular strain of which only grew in the Great High Palace. She was the only person allowed to use this scent. I grew to know it well.

She dismissed her handmaid and then we were alone.

What have you got? she asked.

I had expected her to be eager, but she was so calm. I didn't say anything; I only handed her the bag.

Without a word, she emptied its contents on the ground and picked through the bundles with quick fingers. Like a fishwife but more elegant. I studied her face. Even her stoic mask couldn't conceal her growing excitement.

Did I find the right things? I asked her.

This is everything, she said. *You found his secret records. Everything he wanted to hide . . .*

That's good, I said. That had been my single arrow, my one chance to tear through Chong's room. Imagine if I had only stolen crap. We would be fucked.

How did you get this? she asked as she sorted through it all. *How did you steal all this unnoticed?*

I told her what happened. Every detail. I told her I'd left her device in Chong's hiding place.

And she said, *I see.*

Then she said, *You can't leave here.*

I asked, *You mean I can't leave tonight? Or—*

And she said, *No. I said you can't leave. You have to stay in the palace from now on. You assaulted Chong, a noble. He knows what you've done. Do you think there will be no consequences? He will have you killed. The only place that can offer you enough protection is right here. In the palace. By my side.*

My temper flared. I was so upset—she was the one who got me involved in the first place. I did everything she asked me to, and now she was trapping me in her palace as thanks? I was standing in front of her, like this—and I clenched my fists. Instinct, you know. I think maybe I swore at her, something like *fuck you* or *cheebye,* maybe both.

She laughed. Of course she laughed; I was like an angry child brandishing a stick. Who wouldn't laugh?

I like your spirit, she said.

I asked. *So, what now? Are you going to kill me?*

In my mind, she could do anything she wanted. The easiest way to clean up would be to wipe me from existence. She didn't need me any longer, and then Chong couldn't accuse her of theft or harboring a criminal. I felt that sinking in my gut, you know, the knowledge that you have no hope of escape. I was worth nothing, and I was going to be thrown away like spoiled fruit.

But she looked at me like she was puzzled. *Kill you?* she asked. *Why would I do that?*

You're not afraid I'll cause you trouble? I asked.

I'm not afraid of anything, she said, and I knew that was true. With all her power and cunning, what could she be afraid of?

She said, *You're worried about Chong. You shouldn't be. He is a worm, and I now have everything I need to destroy him.*

But he'll know you were involved in the theft, I said.

Of course, she said. *How could I not let him know who defeated him, when I have won so conclusively?*

Her confidence was intoxicating. It was so easy to get drunk on her. I asked, *Will he really have no recourse against you?*

She smirked and said, *There are things in here that, if released, will get him assassinated in his sleep. Or get him pulled from his cart and beaten to death by ordinary citizens. Do not worry, my darling. He has no hold over us.*

Hearing her say *my darling* and *us* felt so good. I shivered. No one had really cared for me since I left home. No one had looked out for me. We were all too busy looking after our own survival. I had a vision, all of a sudden, of a place where I would be treasured again.

I said, *Can I go back to the dancing house first?*

No, she said. Just as I expected. She said, *It's too late for that now. Leave it all behind. Whatever bonds you forged, they mean nothing now. Whatever possessions you had, they are no longer yours. From today, you are a new person. No longer a simple dancing girl. Your name is ... let's see. I shall name you Lady Han.*

Lady Han! As though I was some kind of nobility! I found the situation absurd. But at the same time, I was thrilled by the idea. Being called a lady by other members of the court! Would some of them start treating me with respect?

She smiled; she touched my face. *You're very brave,* she said. *What you did was extraordinary. I chose right.*

She was so close, and the way she smelled, the way she looked ... it was overwhelming. I'd never felt that way about anyone before. I'd never felt that way about *anything* before.

I asked, *What are you going to do to me?*

And she said, *You mean tonight, or for the rest of time?*

I said, *Both.*

You're going to be my handmaiden, she said. *I need people around me I can trust. Not just to be loyal to me, but also to think for themselves and speak up to me when they feel they need to. You're smart. You have quick wits about you. That's the kind of woman that I like.*

It was flattering, to hear those words coming from

someone like her. I realized how badly I wanted her approval.

She continued: *As for tonight ... well.* She pulled me close, her hands already traveling down my leg. I liked it. I liked it a lot.

She said, *You'll see, won't you?*

Chapter Five

I've been speaking for too long. Time to wet it with another round, let my throat rest. I sure do get through gourds fast when I talk, don't I?

Are you having fun? Are you enjoying this little trip down these rivulets of history? I hope you are, because I won't repeat this shit again. Now it's done, I'll cremate her in my mind, too.

Do I regret the things that happened? Oh, child. Regret's not my thing. Some of what happened was great, and some of it was a bucket of shit. Our land is better in some ways and worse off in others. That's all it is.

Now. Where was I?

Right, so you know how I came to live in the Great High Palace. In a turn of the sun, I was taken from the life I had come to know and plunged into something else. Hekate compared me to a butterfly emerging from a cocoon of misery into something bright and beautiful. She was right, in some ways. What does a butterfly think about its condition? It does not. Its transformation just happens, and the butterfly goes on with life the best it knows how. Then it dies. Luckily for me, I snapped out of the dream before that point. But for now, I was deep in it, stretching my newly dried wings, flitting from one well of nectar to the next.

Hekate was sweet to me. That's a side of her people almost never talk about. Sure, she was cruel, and her tyranny when she became Protector was almost unchecked. But to those she was close to, those she cherished, she could be slow and sweet as syrup. Of course, I was still her servant. I spent my days cleaning up after her and attending to her needs. But she didn't beat me or scold me the way the mamasans in the houses did. The way Madam Wong did. For the first time since I had been taken from home, I found myself treated like another equal person. Treated with *respect*. And that was more intoxicating than these six gourds of wine I've drunk.

Tell me what you want, she said, one early evening as we lay in bed. I told her I wanted to learn slackcraft. It was a crazy idea; I just said it as a joke. I expected her to laugh me down. Instead, she took both my hands and said, *That's a brilliant idea, Little Han! Then you'll be able to protect yourself.* She was so excited, all swept up in emotion like a child.

I didn't think I'd be able to do it. In the villages, you know, nobody could. We thought it was a natural spark. If you had it, you could do it. If you didn't, you couldn't.

And we never met anyone who could. But she told me I was wrong. That the Slack is in everyone, just sleeping . . . Sure, some people will be better than others, some will have better control, some will have more power. It's like running or dancing. You just have to be trained. And she trained me.

Imagine how different the world would be if everyone knew they could learn slackcraft. Imagine if everyone had this awesome, terrifying power.

You learned this too? Where? Out at sea, huh. Who taught you? Your mother? That sounds like I story I'd like to hear. Maybe later.

Alright, alright, I'll continue. Hekate taught me as much slackcraft as she could. It was mostly a wash. I learned a bit of water-nature, a bit of metal-nature, I can lift a cup or shock a cheeky brat. I was a good student, hardworking, but you can't make up for years of not training.

You too? Well, I didn't need any of that fancy Tensor stuff to do what I did. We're good. We've done good.

In any case, life was great. I was so happy. For the first time since I left home, I was comfortable enough to re-lax. No worries about the next day, no stomach-churning cares that bled into restless, sweat-damp nights. I knew nothing bad could happen to me. Hekate was an intox-icating presence, and her power and position hung over me like the bowed fringe of a weeping willow. I enjoyed it all: the fine silks, the gentle perfumes, the bright colors of my surroundings. Was I happy? Hell yes, I was happy. Was it a false happiness? Who the fuck knows. I've never had that kind of untainted joy before or since.

Six months after I moved into the Great High Palace, six months into my newfound state of bliss, the old Protector died.

Now, this wasn't much of a shock. The old Protector hadn't truly been healthy even as a young man, and his health had been deteriorating for years. All that bile finally caught up to him in his fifth decade. Bitter little shit.

Hekate was furious. She'd spent years and years undermining Kamine. The people he grew close to became awfully unlucky. They died in sporting accidents, or their shady dealings got exposed to the public. And this is the upper crust we're talking about—*all* of them were shady. Every last one of those fuckers was corrupt. No one was safe.

If Kamine had even a bit of spine or a vestige of brain, he would have put an end to it. It wouldn't be hard to trace things back to Hekate! That was the worst part of it. She wasn't even being subtle. But Kamine was all *Oh, woe, the fates are cruel to me, what a terrible hand I've been dealt.* Every single time. What a fucking sotong.

Yet despite all her effort, Kamine was to be put on the

throne. For days after her father's death, Hekate vented to me in private, away from prying ears. Why did the old man have to go and kick the bucket when her plans were only halfway through? I listened and nodded sympathetically, but I'd be lying if I said I felt sorry for her. What went through me, instead, was joy and pride. She trusted me! She was telling me things she would tell no one else. I was overwhelmed by her confidence in me, like a sampan swallowed in a tidal wave.

I promised I would do anything to help her achieve her goals. *Tell me how I can help,* I said.

Wouldn't it be nice, she said, *if Kamine simply dropped dead?*

Now. We know that the man was a lazy shitbucket, always overindulging. He only got worse after becoming Protector. Sometimes, he would imbibe so much wine, he wouldn't wake until the next sun cycle. How could such a person run an empire that spans a continent? He can't, that's how. Hekate knew she would have to strike quick and unseen, like a scorpion.

What are you going to do? I asked.

She said, *I'm not going to do anything. Not personally. That's the beauty of it.*

At that time, she was close to another young Tensor, Wang Shaoyun. She had many lovers, but he was one she particularly favored. A researcher, a rising star at the Tensorate Academy. He was ambitious, too, and had his eye on a council post. But it was well known that Kamine didn't like him—some petty grudge from a long time ago. Maybe he didn't like being reminded of his failings. Wang Shaoyun was driven and brilliant and better than Kamine in every way.

Like so many of the hopefuls, he had come to the Great High Palace to pay respects to the old Protector. He was living in the lower quarters for the week. Hekate saw her chance.

I have the perfect job for you, she told me.

My task was simple. In the mornings, the servant types gathered to do the laundry in the great washing room. As a handmaiden, I wasn't expected to do this sort of menial labor. But Hekate made an exception for that day. Wang Shaoyun was particularly close to one of his servants, a girl called Kam. My task was to find her and casually mention, in conversation, that I had overheard Kamine declaring that Wang Shaoyun would never get the post he wanted.

Did he actually say that? I asked.

Hekate said, *No. But she won't know that, will she?*

So, I went to the laundry room. I fit in very well; it had been mere months since I was doing my own laundry, after all. I parked myself next to Kam at the washbasin. *You're Wang Shaoyun's servant, aren't you?* I asked her.

She said yes, so I kept up the inane conversation. Talked about the weather, who had been glimpsed going into whose chambers, that kind of nonsense. This Kam, she was a natural gossip. Once I got her started, I almost couldn't get her to stop.

The moment there was a lull in her conversation, I pounced. I said, *You know, I heard the Protector talk about your master recently.*

That got her attention at once. *What did he say? Oh, you must know my master and the Protector don't get along.*

I pretended I knew nothing. *Oh, they don't?* I said. *That explains why the Protector said those awful things.*

What things? she asked.

Oh, don't think anything of it. He probably didn't mean it. Drunkenly blurted it out at some party or other. Just behind closed doors, to a small handful of people he trusted. Well, except for us servants, I suppose. But we don't count, do we?

What did he say?

Just that he would make sure Kamine never got the post he wants. But, you know. He was only joking. Probably.

I see, she said, and then she went strangely quiet.

I told Hekate what had happened. She seemed pleased. Told me I did a good job.

Do you really think she'll tell Wang Shaoyun what I said? I asked.

Hekate laughed. *The only thing that woman opens more*

readily than her legs is her mouth.

That evening Wang Shaoyun, came to Hekate's chambers in a fit of rage. I left the room to give them a sense of privacy, of course, but through the wood and painted silk of the partitions I could hear his muffled, angry shouting, with Hekate's calm voice interspersed. I don't know what she said to him that night, what subtle insinuations she dropped into his mind like a poison slug. But she was very pleased with the work she did that night. Greeted me the next morning all smiles and pride. Told me how good I'd been.

Wouldn't you know it, months later Kamine simply dropped dead. Took to bed complaining of a headache after having drunk three whole gourds of wine. The next day, he didn't emerge from his room. As expected as the sun rising and falling, right? First sun cycle gone, second sun cycle gone, third sun cycle. By the time the third night cycle came around, people started getting suspicious. His personal maid had been waiting for her summon beacon to hum all day, and nothing. Silence. It was a bit late, even for him. When the sun fell for the fourth time, she decided to check in on him and risk his wrath, just in case. What do you know, she found him all laid out, eyes wide open, so stiff she couldn't even move his arms. He hadn't even taken off his underwear from last night.

What a shock! He'd only been Protector for four months. Obviously, the first thought on everyone's mind was assassination. Someone poisoned him! All the servants in the palace were questioned, their minds and bodies probed by Tensors for the truth. But there was no guilt in any of them. They had performed their duties perfectly.

Meanwhile, the masters of forest-nature, those wise, learned doctors who knew all the workings of the body, had been examining his corpse. They could find no trace of poison in him. His heart had simply . . . stopped. Their conclusion? A natural death. And Sanao Hemana, the new Protector, said, *Alas, my poor cousin. How unfortunate to see his unhealthy lifestyle take hold. We shall all mourn for him.*

Like I said, he wasn't a popular man. Nobody went out of their way to disprove a theory presented by the Tensorate and accepted as truth by the Protector. And anyway, the Tensorate's report *had* been truthful. There were no *detectable* traces of poison in Kamine's body. They didn't lie about that.

Did people think it was suspicious? Of course everyone fucking thought it was suspicious. Do you think people are that stupid? Please. Hekate often had me report how the winds were blowing through the servants' hall, and for weeks they chattered about nothing else. Idle gossip, of course, but if you wanted a forecast of the Protectorate's mood, there was no better place. Servants have lowborn cousins and family, and they slipped between rooms of the elite while they talked amongst themselves, didn't they? The combined knowledge in that hall could have toppled empires. That's the secret, girl—those who serve you, you've got to keep them happy. Take it from me.

There were many theories as to how Kamine died. Some of them were pretty wild, like someone training an animal to smother him, or someone manipulating the nature of fate so that it became inevitable that he would die. What's with your face? People come up with the stupidest ideas. Anyway, the prevailing theory was slack-craft. Some kind of advanced witchery that killed from afar. Maybe some master of forest-nature reached in and stilled the muscles of his heart, just like that. I mean, they weren't crazy. Theoretically, it could have been done. But that degree of control is pretty much impossible, even for the most talented of Tensors. And thank goodness, because can you imagine? Think of how many people would just drop dead. You and I would have died a long time ago.

No. He was poisoned. If the new Protector had wanted to boil the lies off the truth, he would have found out that his late cousin had been taking a new tonic for months, a tonic formulated and produced by a laboratory overseen by Wang Shaoyun. It was really just as simple as that.

So, Hekate got what she wanted. The man she despised, Sanao Kamine, was dead. And in his place, her beloved brother, Sanao Hemana, ascended the throne.

Chapter Six

Ah, Hemana. I've not spoken much about him, have I? He was a man who embodied the phrase "skin of a lamb, heart of a snake." Unlike Kamine, he was a quiet presence in any room. Bookish and soft-spoken. People either trusted him or pitied him, but they didn't see him as a threat. Not until he became Protector, and by then it was too late.

Hekate and Hemana had always been close. He was fifteen years her senior and practically raised her. Both their mothers had died, one after another, and the old Protector had not a nurturing bone in his body. It fell to his older son to look after the wailing infant while his father shut himself in his room, bemoaning the loss of a second wife. That's how he became her caretaker. With his gentle voice and unassuming manner, he taught her hard lessons, about who to trust and who to destroy. Everything she had learned about survival at court, she had learned from him. He had honed her cunning and ruthlessness since she was old enough to walk and talk.

In the brief time I'd been with Hekate, I'd never taken

much notice of him. I never had much reason to. At that time, he headed both the Ministry of Defense and the Ministry of Finance. He was a powerful man and an extremely busy one. He kept counsel with Hekate on long weeknights, but I was not allowed in the room during these sessions. No one else was. His bond with Hekate was sacrosanct and utterly private. Hekate had no quarrel with this. She loved her brother. Idolized the man. And anyway, he was nice to me, his sister's pet. Unfailingly polite, smiled when he saw me, almost made me feel like a human being.

But you know what they say. It's the quiet ones who kill you the fastest. Hemana had reached the summit of power. The world was his. Nothing could hold him back.

The thing about Hemana was that he wasn't cruel. Unlike the many tyrants who litter our nation's glorious history, he took no pleasure in making people suffer, felt no satisfaction from destroying an enemy. Hemana saw the world in dry, logical terms. To him, ruling the Protectorate was simply like a game of xiangqi. If a pawn had to die, if a rook had to be sacrificed, so be it. He would take the offending piece off the board with no more joy than a farmer pulling weeds from their paddies.

The first thing he did was finish what Hekate started: purging what was left of his cousin's power base. He assessed them by the threat they posed and the retaliation he might expect. Some he simply exiled; some he black-mailed into retiring. Others he had killed. One particular administrator in the south—more like a robber baron, re-ally—he didn't just execute. He wiped out the entire family as well. They were prone to revenge killings, and he didn't want any trouble. Then he made the same cold calculation with those who were a threat to him: old enemies, those he didn't like, those who didn't like him. It was brutal, and done within a few weeks. He filled all the vacated spots with his cronies. Within weeks, the power structures of the Pro-tectorate and the Tensorate had been flipped upside down. The Council of Governors—the only ones with enough collective power to resist a Protector's edict—was almost entirely restaffed with those loyal to him.

I asked Hekate if she was worried by what her brother was doing. Manipulating someone into murder was one thing, public executions another. It showed he was a man who had nothing left to fear. *Do you think it might be dangerous?* I asked her.

She simply laughed and said, *This is what a leader does. Watch and learn, my darling.*

I wonder if she ever regretted saying that to me.

Soon after he had ascended to the throne, Hemana sat Hekate down and told her it was time for them to think about their succession. Neither of them had children. *This must change,* he said. *You must find a husband, as I have found a wife.*

Her! Getting married and having children! Of course I wasn't pleased. She had dozens of lovers, and a small handful of confidantes, but a husband? That seemed wrong somehow. I didn't want her to get married. I didn't want her having someone who she could retreat to the shadows with at night or whenever she needed comfort. I didn't want her to have someone else more important than me.

I protested and was met with more laughter. *Don't be foolish,* she said, *of course I must marry. What did you think would happen?*

I hated it, but it made sense. Of course she had to continue her family line. Of course she could not remain unmarried. Of course the strictures of Protectorate society would not part around my new and gleaming reality. In my head, I accepted that this was going to happen, but in my heart, I bled like I'd been stabbed. I couldn't believe that she had caved to her brother's demands so easily.

Yes, I was being ridiculous. Did you think I didn't know that? Who the hell was I? Some servant girl who once did her a favor. A lowborn chit who had been in her life for the blink of an eye. *She* was descended in the direct line of Sanao Chikasu the Conqueror. I just . . .

Give me a moment.

Hekate listened to me. She asked my opinion on things she thought important. She treated me like I mattered. Like—like I was worthy of attention. And love.

But I was determined. She had changed my life, and I would be loyal to her unto death. I let the idea of Hekate having a husband burn me for a few days, and then I forced myself to get over it. So what if she were to be married? A mere husband was nothing. Theirs would be a transactional relationship, existing merely to fulfill a single purpose. It couldn't change what I had with the woman who had become the single most important thing in my life.

Hekate assembled a list of her favorite lovers and a few more eligible highborns she didn't completely loathe. She handed the list to her brother to make a selection. The Protector looked over the list, considered the options, and picked the lucky man who would have her. It was Shaoyun, the poisoner. His part in Kamine's death had already reaped him handsome rewards, and now they were about to get sweeter.

It's a good choice, Hekate told me. *I know his worst secret. We're already bonded.*

See, it was entirely transactional. She didn't see him as a partner. More a necessary evil, one she needed to control.

Still, it was hard to watch her on the wedding dais

all smiles and glowing delight, as if this was what she'd wanted out of life. To be a wife, to sire children for the throne. Surely, she wanted more than that?

That night, after the trials and the tea ceremony and the street parade, there was a lull to allow the bride to change outfits and get ready for the banquet. I was there, helping her out of the ceremonial robes she'd worn, into the sequined dress decorated with so many beads, the fabric strained at its seams. It had taken six royal seamstresses two months to finish it. I'd helped when I could, pricking my thumbs through sunrises and sunfalls. My blood graced the threads of that dress.

She asked me if I was alright. I said, *Well, of course. You look so happy. I'm happy you're happy.*

She said, *This is the best outcome I could have imagined. Things will be different now. But it'll be better. The Protectorate has been sliding into decay for the last three generations. But we're going to change that. I'm excited. Aren't you?*

She said *we.* Those syllables lifted my heart more than anything else ever had.

I said, *I'm excited for the days ahead.* And I smiled, taking her hands in mine.

I swore that I would never let her see my discomfort. I would never show her my petty jealousy, lest she think less of me. This was to be my life now. My future.

Chapter Seven

Hekate fell pregnant four months later. A piece of news that set the whole Protectorate abuzz with joy: an heir to the throne so soon! How unexpected! How fertile the Sanao girl was, unlike her brother's wife, who had four years of marriage with nothing to show for it. The Great High Palace was electric with delight. Geomancers were consulted. A doctor was brought to the Palace to live just a summons away from the mother-to-be.

Personally? I was blindsided by this. Hekate-as-wife led a life almost identical to that of Hekate-as-single-maiden. Wang Shaoyun, now ascendant and very important in the Tensorate, spent all his time away from the Great High Palace. He never took permanent residence in Hekate's chambers, only coming in once or twice a week for conjugal visits and the exchange of useful information. Hekate, meanwhile, had her days packed with meetings and consultations in her new role as the Protector's key adviser. I played the role of messenger and secretary, composing and copying scrolls for her, relaying edicts to lesser administrators. She let me sleep in her bed most nights. An arrangement which pleased me just fine.

Like everyone else, I had assumed that a child would be a long time in coming. After all, Hemana had been married for years and hadn't produced an heir; why should Hekate have been any different? My petty jealousy reared its head again. Surely, a child would unite Hekate and Wang Shaoyun in a way that excluded me.

But I couldn't tell her this. How could I? Hekate glowed at the prospect of motherhood. The tonics she took gave her fine complexion a new radiance, and the fat she put on deepened the beauty she already had. She seemed so thrilled by the idea of having a child to raise.

When this baby is born, Hekate told me, *you'll be its main caretaker while I attend to affairs of state. In this I trust no one more than you.*

What about your husband? I asked.

She laughed for a full minute before she could answer. *Him? Him? That man? As if I would let him take charge of raising* my *child. He's interested in nothing outside his little career.*

It was exactly what I wanted to hear. I drank in this role eagerly, taking charge of preparing for the arrival of a new life. I set up a nursery. I sewed baby clothes. I sent couriers to all the provinces to collect tribute for the royal child to come. If Wang Shaoyun thought he could usurp my place by her side, he was sorely mistaken.

One night, two months before the child was due, I found Hekate sitting quietly in her bedchamber, staring pensively at a calligraphy scroll. Immediately, I knew something was wrong. I went and sat with her, knee to knee, in a way that no one else was allowed to.

She said, *I'm frightened of what's to come.*

How come? I asked. I was surprised. That morning, when I'd seen her in the sunlit gardens, she'd seemed so confident, so sure and happy of the path that had been laid out for her.

Everything's so uncertain, she said. *My brother isn't happy. I wasn't supposed to get pregnant first.*

It made sense that Protector wanted the firstborn heir to be his child. They were the only two left in his generation. The pool of heirs would be small. But he had a four-year head start. I told Hekate as much. If he wanted a child so much, why hadn't he had one yet?

Hekate said, *He's been busy. I was supposed to wait. We did everything right. The slackcraft was supposed to stop my cycles so I wouldn't bear a child. I don't know what happened.*

I'd never seen her this distraught. *It's not your fault,* I told her. *Slackcraft can be fickle. Sometimes it fails.*

She insisted: *It wasn't supposed to fail.*

So, her brother thought she did it on purpose. That

was a dangerous position to be in.

She said, *I think he's angry. He's started using my pregnancy as an excuse to shut me out of meetings and important decisions.*

She said, *I thought there would be no division between us. We're siblings—my child should be as good as his. I don't know what the problem is.*

This vulnerability in Hekate was new to me. So, I said the first thing that came into my head: *If the slackcraft failed, there must have been a reason. I think the fortunes wanted you to have this baby. The child must have some kind of destiny.*

That drew laughter out of her. She said, *I didn't realize you were so spiritual, my darling. You surprise me sometimes.*

But the passage of time cares little for the worries of mortals. The baby grew in her belly and came on time. The labor was as smooth as these things could be, and quick. Everything went as auspiciously as possible. The child was named Nengyuan, a name chosen for good fortune.

The child's arrival seemed to change the Protector's negative attitude. Whenever he had a free moment, he would come to the nursery where I tended the infant. He'd ask me about the child's development, what they had done that day, and so on. Sometimes, he would even hold the child, if he was feeling generous.

Hekate told me, *He sees Nengyuan as his own. We are blood kin, after all.* I supposed that he managed to accept the child's existence, now that they were real.

It was a very busy time. Young children, as you know, require constant supervision. Can't take your eyes off the bastards even for a bit. The infant's parents and parent figures were all busy, so all the fussing and caretaking beyond feeding the brat was left to me. I gladly set aside my former duties as Hekate's administrative assistant. Like my lover had predicted, Shaoyun wasn't interested in raising the child. I never saw him. I suppose he thought he didn't have to worry as long as the child kept breathing. Perhaps he would have taken more of an interest once the child grew old enough to learn slackcraft. We shall never know.

Hekate, at least, adored the child. She was busy, of course; she had a position to maintain! But she made it her duty to spend as much time with the infant as she could. She was there when the baby first rolled onto their stomach and she was there when they learned to stand, wobbling on their chubby legs. Imagine, if you will, two young women laughing in a sun-dappled room while a baby babbles in their arms. If you had asked me about the future back then, I would have painted a pretty picture of a family blossoming. Of Hekate and I walking down a peaceful, shaded path together, having left the horror and darkness of the last few years behind. I was so sure this joy would last forever.

It's strange, knowing what I know now, being the person I am now, to recall how *human* she seemed during that time.

As with all things concerning that place and that person, it couldn't last. I remember: it was the day of Nengyuan's first birthday. One year of watching this squalling creature go from a barely sentient worm to something almost like a human. I'd sewn a new outfit for their birthday. Stayed up all night finishing it. Red silk with golden threads, festooned with motifs of the four celestial beasts: dragon, phoenix, tiger, and horse. I'd been looking forward to seeing them wear it.

I woke to a scream, the blade-sharp sound of grief. It was Hekate. I'd been sleeping in the next room—I'd stayed up late, and my lamplight would have disturbed the child. I stumbled from my bed and ran into the nursery.

At some point in the night, the child had died.

I don't remember much of that day, or that week. Wish I did. Wish I spent more time observing and analyzing how everyone dealt with it. I don't remember the Protector's exact reaction. Or Shaoyun's. Not that it would have made much difference. Or *any* difference. Not to what happened afterward. But I like to have my references in my head, my records. You know what I mean? You know?

If you've ever gone through something like that ... no, what am I saying, of course you have. Fuck. It takes everything out of you. All the energy, all the reasoning, all the meaning. You had something, and all of a sudden, it's gone. It's so hard to understand.

Hekate was ... well, she was broken. Devastated. Of course she was! Her firstborn, her child that she had carried within her for months, the child into whom she had poured so many of her hopes and dreams. Taken from her in a single cruel, incomprehensible blow.

But Hekate's not the kind to lie in a dark room, weeping into her sleeves. Even in her terrible sorrow, she was angry. Burning with rage. Her fire is not like the kind that sweeps forests and leaves only ashes behind. It's the kind that burns underground, hollowing out the ground from under you. It's the kind of anger that's like lava, a force of nature that reshapes the world. Don't think you can break her with sadness; she'll come for you every time.

I shouldn't talk about her like she's still alive.

Mere weeks after that, Shaoyun died. It was said he succumbed to a broken heart, drank himself to death chasing his child. Hekate refused to believe it any more than when the doctors had said Nengyuan had died of natural causes. The timing of both deaths was a bit too convenient.

She told her brother as much. I was in her chambers when she lost her temper, a rare occasion where she raised her voice to him. *This is an attack on our family—on your family!* she said. *Will you let this stand? We must find these perpetrators and make sure justice is meted out. Harshly, so that no one thinks they may strike our family and live!*

But her brother took her aside. Gently holding her hands in his he said, *Dearest sister, my sweet Hekate, the sorrow burdened upon you has been great. But you have let your grief drive you mad. You are seeing things where there is nothing! What happened to Nengyuan was a tragedy, but one that is all too common. Children are so vulnerable at this age! Do you not remember what happened to our cousin Sushila, who passed before they were six months old? And poor, poor Shaoyun, to follow his child after! He was such a sensitive soul. To lose him this way—what a blow to the Tensorate. What a blow to all of us.*

I cannot let the same to happen to you, he told her. *I cannot lose you as well. You must get better, Hekate. You must recover from these wounds upon your heart.*

Hekate quieted at his words. But after he was gone, she turned to me, her anger renewed. She said, *I know who did it now.*

I was surprised by this. *Who?* I asked.

She spat: *Lian.*

Lian was Hemana's wife. They had been married since long before I came on the scene. She was willowy and delicate as the flower she was named after, with roots as thick and murky. Twenty years old, skilled in all the relevant arts, no prospects other than to be bartered for familial prestige. Like all the highborn women I knew, she was excellent at concealing herself behind silk screens of modesty and politeness.

I was naturally shocked by Hekate's conclusion. Lian had always been cordial to us. She asked after me every now and then, took the trouble of learning my name, and I was on good enough terms with her maid, Aisha, that the girl even helped out with the cleaning and washing when Nengyuan got to be too much.

Lian was a quiet girl, distant from everyone. But during the pregnancy and after the birth she retreated into herself. She hardly left her wing of the palace. I never saw her call on Hekate after Nengyuan's birth, even as her husband spent more and more time with his sister and heir-to-be.

Hekate said, *She didn't show her face at either of the funerals. She hasn't sent condolences. I know it's her.*

I said, *I understand she has reason to hate you—after all, her sole job was to produce a royal heir, and you did it first. I'm sure she resents you. But someone like her? I cannot imagine she could do something like this.*

What I meant was: This girl is a mere fox, she cannot roar like a tiger. How could something so timid and retiring strike at the Protector's own sister?

Hekate said, *You don't know her whole situation like I do. She's been under immense pressure since I conceived. Her one duty as the wife, and she failed? She didn't just shame herself; she shamed her family name. You can't imagine the kind of judgment she's getting from her entire family. From all of Protectorate society. She loathes me for doing this to her. This is her revenge.*

I trusted Hekate's intuition completely. If she said so, it must be true.

I said, *There's one way to know for sure.*

So, just like old times, she sent me to Lian's room to ferret out the proof. Called Lian away from her quarters in the evening, gave me a couple of hours with which to work. The woman's room was protected by warding spells, of course, and servants weren't supposed to have slackcraft ability. But I wasn't an ordinary servant, was I? It took me no effort to disarm the warning system, dissipating the threads of slackcraft strung across the door.

I searched her room. I found her private diaries, and they were exceedingly dull reading: full of angst but empty of murderous intent. Not the slightest clue of treason and betrayal. Just the dregs of a sad, frustrating life and a woman too soft to do anything about it.

Then I got to the last few months of entries, and found them written in a code I could not read.

This is it, I thought.

I couldn't steal the entire diary without being found out. So, I lifted pages, undoing the binding and pulling a good chunk of sheets from the beginning of the coded part. This was what I brought back to Hekate.

Under lamplight, Hekate took one look and said, *This is the women's hand.* It was an archaic system of writing developed hundreds of years ago and mostly fallen out of use but kept as tradition in some noble families. No wonder I couldn't read it.

But Hekate could, and the first few pages she read drew a gasp. *She was pregnant,* she said. Her astonishment turned quickly to anger. *See! This is why she killed my child! My husband! She wanted to get rid of the competition!*

She flipped through the rest of it. Her frustration grew. *There's nothing here! No plans, no intents! Just . . . her stupid hopes and dreams. Are you sure you got everything?*

I said, *Of course I didn't take everything, I was trying not to get caught! I left the last month or so still in the book.* I gritted my teeth. I'd thought I was being *smart,* not taking everything.

Hekate said, *Looks like you have to go back and get it, don't you?*

But that didn't happen. See, what I didn't realize at that time was that the Palace was under constant attack. Rebels in the southern regions had been sending assassins. The rebels needed to destabilize the country to break free of their chains, and a death in the Protector's family might do that for them. But the assassins, skilled as they were, still couldn't get past the slackcraft wards in the palace.

Guess who just disrupted one?

They were so fast. They must have been sending a dozen assassins every night. I broke into Lian's room in the evening, right before the first night cycle, and by the second sunrise of the night cycles, she was dead. No one had time to spot and repair the broken threads that would have killed an intruder and set off the alarm. I killed her.

I was certain I was doomed. The assassins had been able to break in because while I tried to restore the protections around Lian's quarters, I did a shit job of it. I'd never been trained! Skilled Tensors would be able to figure out who had been the culprit. I'd been caught with my ass unwashed, and small people like me are the first to be broken on the spearpoints of history and discarded by the powerful. I was sure Hemana would never forgive me for what I had done. Maybe he would not even forgive his sister.

Hekate told me, *Don't worry. You wait here for me. I will sort this out.*

Her jaw was steel and her eyes were the red of a forge. Even with all the turmoil around us, she was so steady. So calm. No typhoon could move her. God, I loved her.

She gathered the pages I had stolen from Lian's room and set off to confront her brother.

After about an hour, the summons beacon in my pocket lit up. I'd been quietly trembling in Hekate's quarters, and I thought, *This is it. Here comes the end.* I followed the charm's glow to the Protector's private chambers.

Hekate was in that room. So was the Protector, but not seated in the judgment I expected. He was dead, and she was holding the knife.

She hadn't shown him any mercy. He lay on the ground like a gutted fish, cut from collarbone to navel. The floor looked like a slaughterhouse.

He did it, Hekate hissed.

I was speechless. A murder! She'd just committed a murder! Why? I didn't understand her words at all. I thought she meant that he'd killed Lian, but even that thought was meaningless nonsense. I just stood there, blinking like an idiot.

I can't believe it, she said. *My own brother. How could he do that to me?*

That got through the thick molasses of my brain. She

meant Nengyuan! Her brother had murdered her child. All the time we wondered who might have reason to have the baby killed, we never suspected their uncle. Of course. Of course. The firstborn of every generation inherits the throne. Lian was pregnant, a fact that he hid from us. He wanted the next Protector to be his own child.

I thought we were flesh and blood, Hekate said. She might have been crying, I don't remember. My brain was like dumb cabbage. My memories got saved all slanted and skewed. Just fragments here, fragments there. She said—she said, *I thought there were no divisions between us. I thought—my good was his good—*

No, she was definitely crying. I remember the way my shoulder got wet.

No, you're thinking about it wrong. I didn't say anything to solve the puzzle for her. How did she find out? He told her. It turns out she bloody turned me in. Just straight-up said, *I had my girl break those wards because I thought Lian killed my son and my husband.* And he said, *You fool, it was me who did it.*

Ironic, isn't it? She trusted him so much. She thought he would listen to her, forgive her for Lian's death, if only she told the truth. And she never imagined that he could do something like kill her child. All for his own vanity.

She thought he was wise enough to accept her child

as the logical heir to the throne. But he had not. She had never mattered to him as a person. All he saw in her was a tool. Someone who was perfectly loyal to him, someone whom he could use. She was smart and strong and one of the most talented Tensors in the land, even more than he was. She had been doing his dirty work for years.

So, she killed him. That was her true nature, rearing up when provoked. I don't think he expected that. I don't think he expected his own dear sister to turn against him that way. Fool. He didn't understand her at all. She fought him, and she won. As I said, she was strong. And once he was dead, once his limbs had stopped thrashing and the light had fled from his eyes, she called for me. Her trusted servant. The one person left in the world she could rely on. And dutifully I came.

All these years, she said, *I thought I knew him. But I never did. And now I never will.*

I looked at the body in front of me. A third dead Protector before the ink on seals had time to dry. What would people say?

What happens now? I asked her.

Now, she said. *Now I am in charge.*

Chapter Eight

Of course it wasn't that simple. Of course there were consequences for killing a Protector. If it were that simple, none of them across history would have lasted a month. Before she could take control and reshape the world, Hekate went on trial for the murder of her brother.

Back then, there was a council of senior magistrates who handled the most serious cases in the land. They were empowered to pass judgment on anyone, even the Protector themselves. The High Council, they were called. They had been around for several dynasties. And sure, they were mostly ceremonial in cases involving the Protector, because who else put them in their positions? This situation was different, though. Hekate might have been the Protector by name, by rule of law, but she was a usurper to the throne. Her hands were stained with the blood of the man who put them in their positions. I don't know if they had a plan for after they got rid of her and ended the line of the Conqueror—who did? During those months, it was all chaos, all the time. I only know they hated her.

They imprisoned Hekate in her chambers and set a trial date. Five days. A short call, but the Protector was the axis around which the empire spun, and without someone in that position, it was all coming apart, very quickly. As her servant, I was the only one allowed to see her. I would bring her food, clean her room, bring her news of the outside world. I was there when the call arrived, and I watched her shoulders set. We knew that also meant they had already made up their mind.

Hekate said she wanted a public trial. Five days was enough for administrators from all over the Protectorate to travel to the capital. And she wanted citizens of every class to be able to watch.

Of course, said the High Council, *let everyone bear witness.* They saw her as a soft, naive girl. They were eager to doom her before an audience of the entire Protectorate.

I thought she was crazy. She was risking so much. But she never did anything halfway. And this was her life, her history, her legacy at stake. I asked her, *Are you sure about this?*

She told me, *Don't worry. This is my plan.*

The day of the trial came around. It felt like spring, that festival energy in the air, you know? The streets packed with people, the gossip, the smell of food cooking. The trial was held at the grand pavilion square in front of the Great High Palace, the place that had that year seen two coronations and three funerals. Hekate was calm. The High Council sat on a dais specially constructed for this occasion. Thousands packed the square. Thousands more filled the space around the Great High Palace. In those days, they didn't have the technology to broadcast to distant places as they do today. Otherwise, more could have watched it.

The audience was just what she wanted.

The High Council set to work. It was obvious that Hekate had killed her own brother, the Protector. All the evidence pointed that direction. There were witnesses, the guards at the door, the servant who found us there. She didn't deny it. They laid out their case and said, *The punishment for this crime should be death.*

And then it was Hekate's turn to defend herself, as was the right of the accused.

She knelt before the dais. There were Tensors there to amplify her voice so it could be heard across the city. She was ready.

It was decades ago, but that memory stays as clear in my mind as a light capture. How small she looked. How human and fragile, a young girl set against the backdrop of the hungry crowd, the steel-eyed men set to judge her. Yet how unafraid she looked. How unbowed.

She said, *My brother killed my son. I had to avenge my little boy. So, I killed the man who had him murdered. If it is justice to kill a murderer, and murder to spill royal blood, then I carried out justice.*

There was shock. The crowds watching gasped.

One of the councilors said, *And what proof do you have of that?*

And so, she summoned me.

See, when she called me to the Protector's chambers that fateful day, it wasn't just idle fancy. She wanted to give me something.

Hekate had sneaked a light capture device into her robes. She *always* recorded everything that happened in high-level meetings, and this time was no different. He should have known that. Maybe he thought she trusted him enough to make a mistake. When I came to the room, she gave the device to me. And it was that recording that I played for the High Council and the gathered crowd. They saw Hemana say, with his own mouth, *I was the one who killed your son.*

You can only imagine the reaction. How unforgivable of him! How cruel! How little remorse he showed! Of course she would have reacted the way she did. It was only natural. Only a mother's instinct.

I was there; I felt the shock in the crowd. The raw anger. There were mothers in the crowd, parents, people who loved their parents. The parental bond is such a primal force, isn't it? People understood at once. It wasn't murder—it was punishment! Justice! How powerful her love for the son she lost, that it drove her to do such things. The light capture turned her act of slaughter into something noble. Something heroic. Tragedy to answer tragedy, the only possible response after her own brother delivered such a blow.

The High Council was doomed the moment the light capture began to play. For them to condemn Hekate while the public felt so strongly for her would have caused outrage. The mob would murder them on the spot for their injustice! Given the choice between suicide and absolution, they absolved her.

For their wisdom, Hekate rewarded them handsomely. She didn't have them executed when she disbanded the Council. I suppose they were grateful, but I don't waste much time imagining their feelings. The story doesn't end with their disposition.

That light capture was not just an absolution for Hekate's actions. It was also a warning to those who would be her enemies, and those who hadn't decided if they would oppose her. That light capture said, *See how swiftly she moves, see how unstoppable she is! This is not a woman to be tangled with; this is not a woman you want to anger. She will show you no mercy. She will come for you, and she will not stop until you are dust.*

After all—if she could take the blade to her own brother, the man who raised her, the person she was closest to in the world, who *wouldn't* she kill? Who wouldn't she sacrifice to her wants and her ambitions?

That tumultuous month was her turning point. She became the Protector, yes, but not only by ascending the throne. She also became the woman we know as the Protector. See, before this, she was just like any other highborn Tensor. A shitbucket through and through, but one who still had a soft, human core. A woman with weaknesses, who would succumb to those weaknesses on occasion. Someone whom you and I could understand, someone whose feelings I could understand. The Hekate who emerged from that trial . . . was not that kind of person. My lover was gone; I just hadn't realized. I wouldn't realize for many years.

I can never trust again, she said one night as we lay in bed. *Under the right circumstances, even the most loyal and loving dog will turn and bite you. Even the most trustworthy person will betray you. And I will not suffer the wounds of another such surprise.*

I will never betray you, I said. And I'll tell you, at that moment, I believed it truly and sincerely. I loved her so much, and I had so much sympathy for her and anger at what she'd been put through. I wanted to protect her. I wanted to be by her side forever.

She laughed. *Even you, my precious peony. Even you will turn against me when the time is right.*

I thought, *You're wrong. You're wrong about me. You don't see how much I love you. I'm the closest one to you now; I'm the one who knows you best. You need me. I'll never betray you. You'll see.*

Lying there with her breath against my skin I vowed that I would the one who would be the most devoted, the most trustworthy, the most truthful right hand she could have. I would prove her wrong. I lived for her.

Chapter Nine

Hekate knew she was in a precarious position. Lian's murder and the subsequent mess had done exactly what the southern rebels had wanted: it had wrecked the structure of the Protectorate and put everything into chaos. She knew that if the empire she ruled were to survive, she would have to act swiftly and decisively. She could not purge the administration as her brother had done. Not again. For one thing, her brother had killed or disposed of hundreds of perfectly competent officials and Tensors. She didn't have the numbers to replace his appointments and run a functional bureaucracy. Also, she didn't have a ready-made network of cronies like her brother did. His network had been *her* network. They'd built it together, and it had all been compromised.

So, she had to be selective, but she wasn't secretive. She said, *I am going to change the structure of the Protectorate. I am consolidating my power, and you can either stand with me, or against me. There will be no cracks and divisions in the Protectorate I am building. It will be strong, it will stand, it will not fall.*

First of all, she tested the loyalty of the royal guards. These were pugilists from the Grand Monastery, with whom she had a good relationship. They were meant to be above politics, leaving such trivial matters behind in the pursuit of spiritual purity and oneness with the Slack. Hekate asked them to leave their monastic order to serve her. Leaving the order was as big a deal back then as it is now. The pugilists had been initiated as children. They had dedicated their entire lives to the monastic way. To leave the order was more than leaving family behind. It was rejecting their entire identities.

Yet a large number of them still left. Maybe a third. Some of them were swayed by what she offered them: wealth and a life away from the austere strictures of the Grand Monastery. Others were loyal to her, to what the throne of the Protectorate represented. This was the seed of the schism between the Grand Monastery and the Great High Palace. She split them apart. From then on, the Protectorate no longer relied on the Grand Monastery for royal guards; the defectors trained new recruits. Hekate cared little about the thousands of years of tradition she was destroying. All she wanted was a compact, loyal force of soldiers to reshape the face of the Protectorate with.

With this small army at her back, her next step was to get rid of all the governing councils, ministry elders, and the like. In this Hemana had trained her well. She sweet-talked, she blackmailed, and of course she intimidated. But she was crafty about it, more cunning than her brother, even. She didn't simply execute the deposed bureaucrats wholesale—there is a fine line between being a tyrant that is feared and a tyrant that is hated, and she didn't want to cross it. On the other hand, she could not leave them be to plot against her, couldn't let them live in the city with all their wealth and contacts, simmering with resentment. So, she generously allowed them the chance to leave for the provinces with their lives and the clothes on their backs. The younger ones were to take elixirs that would render them barren, stemming the possibility of children coming back for revenge.

Many of them refused this fate, preferring to die with their dignity intact. They had spent their lives serving the Protectorate, they were old; were they supposed to build new lives as common peasants? Letting a few martyr themselves was fine with Hekate. It was their *choice,* after all.

In the wake of that carnage, Hekate shaped the Protectorate that you now know—the ministries grouped under three pillars with an overseeing consul for each one, and the Tensorate folded in as the fourth pillar. She had ambition fit for a dozen people, and in her chamber with her scrolls and ink, she envisioned a completely new society structured to her particular whims.

Was it brilliance? Was it madness? Well, both of them are states of mind, aren't they? It depends on who's telling the story. What is called madness in one mouth is called brilliant in another. The mad who succeed and win love—or at least little hatred—are remembered as simply brilliant.

Which one was it for Hekate? I'm the one telling the story. I say it was both. She was mad, but her madness was also brilliance. For good or for ill, she changed the Protectorate forever.

Of course, it all sounds *easy* when I talk about it like this. As though she waved a hand and the rest of the Protectorate fell into place. But you know that's not how it happens. Oh, you know. You can imagine the dark things that happened in the cracks covered by these pretty pictures. The knives in the night. The children orphaned. The blood washed out before the light of the next sunrise. When the threads of fortune change direction, how many are caught in the trap of their weaving? How many are strangled or have their throats cut?

I spent those years as a spy, or whatever you want to call it. I did whatever she needed me to do. The stuff she wouldn't let anyone else touch because it was too sensitive. I carried out special missions. Broke into houses. Learned martial arts from ex-pugilists. Oh, I learned so much in those days. The art of subterfuge. Ways to be invisible at the right times. How to threaten a man without lifting a finger. Everything I am now, everything I did as the leader of the Machinists, I learned in those days.

There was no word for what I was. I was not her lover, although we were lovers; I was not her confidante, even if she held me in confidence; I was not her advisor, even when she sought my advice. A new hierarchy was solidifying around her, but I had no official place in it.

Yet I enjoyed it. There was a freedom in being beholden to no one but her. I would do anything she asked me to, and I was proud of it.

I remember the first time I killed a man. He was just a servant, coming in to clean his master's room in the cloudy murk of a night-cycle. And there I was, a stranger all wrapped in black, fingers prying apart boxes that held his master's secrets. I saw him draw breath and open his mouth to call the whole house down on me. Before I thought, I cut his throat, from here to here. Blood all over. Good thing the floors were very expensive wood, very well laid, no gaps in between. Rich folks' floors are so easy to clean. And he already had buckets and rags with him. Hiding his body was the hardest part. I took his clothes and hid the bloodstains with some of my black scarves. From afar, in the dark, you'd have thought me just another servant of the house. I had just enough slackcraft to help me carry the body. I buried him outside the grounds.

You know what part still fucks with me? The household didn't notice he was gone until a week later. His brother came looking for him after he didn't show up for a meeting. The servants thought he'd been sent home. The masters didn't care. A whole person, missing for a week, and nobody noticed.

They never found the body. The household thought *he* stole the things I took and ran. Sold it for a handsome profit to the Protector, who used it to blackmail. All while his bones rotted in the soil an arrow's flight away.

Once you've ended someone's existence forever, you're never the same. There was nothing left I wouldn't do. I killed for Hekate again. And again, and yet again. I didn't *enjoy* it, mind you. I'm not a demon. But I didn't lose any sleep, either. Why should I? I thought I was doing the right thing.

Don't raise your eyebrows at me, child. You think the Protectorate you know is rotten and corrupt? You should have seen it as it was, before Hekate cleaned it up. Sure, she was cruel and vindictive, and sure, many have suffered under her rule. But many more suffered in the years before she came to the throne. Would you look at the peasants who are no longer starving, or the women who have the choice to live as they please, and tell them that they do not deserve what they have today? If a few drops of blood had to be spilled along the way, so be it. It's like a game of xiangqi, after all. Sacrifices have to be made. Your conscience is clean, that's great. Mine isn't. And I've learned to live with that.

Chapter Ten

Kanina. There isn't enough wine in this place. Not enough wine in the whole world.

Please. Don't tell me about my liver. Do I look like someone who cares about her health? I came here to get drunk. That's what I'm doing.

Hmm. I left eventually, of course. How did I do it? Or why? I...

Look. I was with her for a really long time, alright? Decades. I watched her crush the two southern rebellions and the Tsing uprising in the capital. You remember that, huh? Were you even walking then?

Oh, so your mother told you. Yes. It was over forty years ago. How old do you think I am?

Hah! I'm flattered, but no. I'm much older than that. Hekate, you know, longevity was one of her research interests, on top of... other things. We took all these elixirs when I was younger. I guess they worked. She could have lived past a hundred, I guess, if the bomb hadn't gotten her. Heavens, I hope that's not my fate, to live that long. I fear it may well be. I don't know what she did to herself, or what *more* she did to me. Oh, that would be a fine last revenge on her part. I fucking hope not. I can't take another thirty years in this cursed existence.

Fine. You want to know how I turned from Hekate's most loyal lieutenant to her greatest enemy? I can tell you that part, too. It won't make you like me any better, I assure you.

The wild ride that started Hekate's rule slowed over the years as the tempests of upheaval eased. She had learned to control the ocean, and no longer cared about the waves. Around her, the Protectorate grew steady and strong in the patterns she determined for it. Sure, there were uprisings every now and then, little eruptions of discontent here and there. But putting out those little fires was nothing. Most of the provincial rebellions mussed nary a hair in the capital.

With the calming of the situation, Hekate had much less need for me to do the dirtier parts of my job. Increasingly, I found myself handling paperwork, maintaining lists of informants and those who had earned Hekate's trust—or ire. Hekate was busy, I was busy. The passion of our early years faded with the unrest that had fueled it.

About ten years into her regime, Hekate started thinking about heirs again. The wounds inflicted by Nengyuan's death had healed into silver scars. She told me, *I will never marry again. Who needs a husband to continue the family line? Not me.*

Again, she was very methodical about it. For a stud she chose a young Tensor who was promising in all the right ways—clever and gifted in slackcraft, but with zero ambition and the personality of a wet noodle. She didn't want him leveraging his paternity, see. His name was—what was it? Liao. Liao Jing, that was it. Her first four children were sired by this man, until he died in a mysterious accident. Drowned while on vacation to the south coast. Maybe it really was an accident. Maybe. Anyway, I had nothing to do with it, so my conscience is clean.

Yet Hekate kept producing children after his death. After Tamiya, Chunling, Yaoshun, and Kohana came Deryang, Mie, and Sonami. Sonami was going to be her last, she said. She didn't need any more. Seven children were enough for her to secure the future of the Protectorate. She would train them from birth to succeed her when she finally left this existence for good.

Court gossip assumed there was a second person—or a series of people—responsible for the last three children. But I knew of no such thing, and at that time, I thought I knew all her secrets. I didn't, of course. You'll see in a bit. But what I *did* know was that soon after her coronation, Hekate started a unit of the Tensorate that was so secret, only a handful of people knew it existed. That secret unit was tasked with research into human reproduction. I fully believe they finally developed a way to create children with only one parent. To make perfect copies of Hekate, so to speak. It's been remarked upon that the last three of the Protector's children look very much like each other, hasn't it? Especially that Sonami. A devil's replica of her mother at all stages of her life.

Hekate became very involved in the management of her children's lives. She left the weaning to wet nurses, but once they were old enough to walk and talk, they became her sole property. A far cry from the days when she and I would clear time—one afternoon a week—to play with Nengyuan. No point to it except the pure delight on a child's face, untainted by the blemishes of the world around them.

Around that time, I started thinking about having children of my own. It started as a string of idle thoughts that wound its way through my mind as I lay awake reminiscing, and grew steadily until it was a burning that consumed me day and night. Maybe it was the act of growing older; maybe it was watching Hekate recede even further from me as she surrounded herself with her children. Her hope for the future. What would be *my* legacy? What would I leave behind when I was gone? My thoughts turned again and again to the family I had been taken from as a tender child. I remem-

bered how my sister Xiuqing had given me that jade elephant, the most precious thing she owned, as a going-away
present. I'd abandoned that trinket—along with everything
else—in the dancing house that fateful night when Hekate
made me hers.

I wondered how my family was, what they were doing,
if they thought of me at all.

I started hiring bed-partners to get me pregnant.
Boldly enough, I didn't ask Hekate for permission to do
this. I was my own woman, after all. I thought: *I've given
so much of my life to her. My loyalty has earned me the right
to choose the path of my future.*

Several years passed, with no result. There was an uprising in the capital. The Grand Monastery was recruited
to help quash it. The Protector's final pair of children—the
twins—were born and packed off to the mountains as a
blood price. Still my womb remained barren as the desert
plains of the north. I had been trying, and trying, and trying. Nothing worked.

I didn't want to approach Hekate with this. We had
drifted apart enough that it would be embarrassing. It
wasn't like the old days anymore when we were both tender, fiery girls.

But my desperation grew. I knew that children would
be harder to come by with age. I was running out of time.

Finally, I could stand it no more. I had hoped that

Hekate would sense something was wrong and come to *me* and ask. But she didn't, and the desire within me was so strong, I could no more hold it back than I could a storm river. I went to her private chambers, which I no longer slept in, and said, *I need help from your Tensors.*

She said: What for?

I told her, *I'm having trouble conceiving. I know your secret unit can help me. I want children.*

She looked at me for a long, cold moment. And then she laughed.

Oh, my darling Han, she said. *I thought you would have it figured out by now. The years have dulled your wits, I see.*

I didn't understand what she meant. I was confused, hurt. Like a baby.

She said, *You are barren, my dear. No amount of slack-craft will undo the damage caused to your womb by the elixirs you took all those years ago.*

What elixirs? I asked, confused.

She said, *The ones I laced your food with.*

How can I describe the blade of betrayal that vivisected me in that moment? The shock, the dizziness, the pain? All I could muster was a *What, why?*

She said, *I didn't want you having children. I thought they would distract you from your purpose.*

I said, *So, you fed me elixirs without my knowledge? The*

same elixirs you were feeding to your enemies? You poisoned me!

She said nothing. She was unapologetic. She had never truly apologized for anything she had done in her life, and she was not about to start.

You know what the worst thing is? She could have just asked me to stay childless. I would have done it for her. Gladly.

But she didn't want to ask me. She didn't trust my loyalty. She just took away my ability to have a child. She took away my choice.

That was when I knew she had never seen me as an equal, she never would. Fuck, she didn't even see me as fully human. She was a dictator, and this is how dictators treated those under them.

Our relationship had meant nothing to her.

I suppose I always knew this. I had been in denial. For years. Years! I deluded myself! I thought she at least cared for me. I thought she appreciated me as the person who had been with her through the worst moments of her life, as the one person who had never doubted her, as the person who had kept her secrets for decades. But I was wrong. She was, after all, the woman who had killed her own brother on her way to becoming Protector. The woman who told me plainly that she would never trust another person, and had laughed at me when I said, *Trust me.*

Why didn't I believe her when she told me?

I wanted to lash out so badly. I wanted to kill her where she stood. But my years as her spy and assassin had honed my instincts and my self-control. I knew that attacking her would be futile. I would die on the spot, and what then? Would she even shed any tears over my death? Or would she triumphantly say, *I was right,* and then go on with her life?

No. If I was to die, I would give her hell before I did.

I went back to my quarters. I pretended to be angry for a few days, then pretended to forgive her. I told her she was right to do what she did. That she was infinitely wise. That of course my body and my future were hers to do with whatever she wished.

I hid my resentment and let it burn like an old mine fire. I looked and looked for ways to exact my revenge.

Now. In the north of the Protectorate, the exiled Tensor Shao Weiyi had been cultivating the new movement he called Machinism. He had been helping peasants to build machines that could do what Tensors did, but by using mundane principles, free of slackcraft. Word of his work had been spreading in the rural areas, and rumbles of it were reaching the capital. It was a movement that was starting to gain enough support to annoy Hekate.

Shao Weiyi, the leader of the movement, had retreated into the mountains in the north and begun spreading word to his supporters all over the Protectorate from there. He would send forbidden materials into villages, the local authorities would confiscate them, and a small, angry uprising would break out. Hekate would quash a rebellion in one village only to have another spring up. It was wearing on her. She wanted the problem obliterated, once and for all.

She told her pugilists that she wanted Shao Weiyi captured. End him, and his little movement would be over.

Over the next few months, her people caught many prominent Machinists, closing in on Shao Weiyi's inner circle. I processed all the paperwork. It was just one scroll after another in my usual daily pile, and I paid it very little mind. Trivial. Trivial stuff. And then, one day, something in a report snared my attention.

The pugilists said they had caught the woman codenamed Yellow Tiger. She was a big deal, rumored to be Shao Weiyi's lover. The report said that the pugilists had ambushed her in a village north of Jixiang, her hometown that she returned to every so often. They burned the village after.

I hadn't heard that name in years. The village of my birth. I got chills. Jixiang was small enough everyone knew everyone. And it had been many years since I'd lived there, but I knew for certain that Yellow Tiger's capture had cost the lives of people I had known and shared meals with, or their children. Hekate had burned down anything that was left of my past, my family.

At the bottom of the report was the woman's age and her real name.

I stood. I was very quiet. I made some preparations for myself. Then I went down to the cells where the important prisoners were kept.

She recognized me at once. Decades had passed and we were grown women, white hairs coming in, but we knew each other without question. Xiuqing. My sister. She cried out my birth name, which had not been used since I left home and has not been used since.

I wanted to rush to her, to break the slackcraft barrier that kept her imprisoned. I could not believe it. After all these years, she was here, and under these circumstances.

Why are you here? she asked. *Why are you dressed like this—like one of them?*

I work for the Protector, I said. *I'm her right-hand woman.*

Xiuqing was horrified. *How could you serve her?* she asked. *She's a murderer, a tyrant! The things she's done are unforgivable. She has the blood of hundreds on her hands. Thousands! She murdered our family. They burned down the village. Everyone is dead!*

I said, *Shut up.* I didn't want her making a scene. Emotions were running wild through me, but I kept my composure.

I told the guards, *The Protector has asked me to bring this prisoner to her.*

They nodded. That was completely within reason.

I pointedly undid the slackcraft barrier in front of Xiuqing. I didn't want her getting any ideas.

I restrained her hands and led her through the Palace. She hissed and spit invective at me. Called me a disappointment, a traitor, a monster with no conscience. All the way down the long corridors, past the colorful pavilions and the gilded pillars.

I kept saying, *Be quiet. Move. Stop shouting.*

The fewer people took notice of us, the better.

She only understood what I was doing when we came to the courtyard with all the slackcraft carts. *You're helping me escape?* she asked.

Shut up, I said. And then added, *I'm coming with you.*

We stole one of the carts. In my robes were stashed a few key things: maps and ledgers, mostly. Nothing of sentimental value. I had learned the hard way that sentimentality did you no good. On our way out, before we got to the outskirts of the city and dumped the cart and became fugitives officially, my sister and I exchanged our stories. She told me about the years that had ground her down, the hardships that had befallen our village.

My brothers' death in an unfortunate accident. My parents' sickness and grief. The new administrators sent after Hekate's purges, cruel and hard, who demanded more tribute from the village than they could afford. The hunger and the despair. And then Shao Weiyi, who came to the village with devices—machines!—that would help them irrigate the paddy fields, lift heavy objects, wash and grind rice. And it wasn't just that. He provided tonics to heal the soil, which you could brew with mundane powders. Medicines for small ailments. He told them that they, too, could learn these small magics. They were not magics at all. Anyone could perform them.

She left the village to be with him. The Machinist movement became her life.

I, too, told her what had happened to me. Much as I told the story to you. Maybe I left out some of the worst parts. I wanted her to like me, to trust me. I emphasized how much of Hekate's life I had been privy to. How much of the Protectorate's inner workings I understood.

Xiuqing said, *I forgive you for the things you have done. She made a fool of you, after all. Manipulated you and lied to you. You are just as much a victim in this story as I am.*

I'm not a victim, I told her.

She agreed because she didn't understand what I was saying. *No,* she said, *we are not. We are survivors. Look at us: two sisters, consorts to the rival leaders in this fight, now reunited. This cannot be coincidence.*

This is the doing of the fortunes, I said. It sounded nice. The kind of sentimental thing people like to hear. I said, *This was meant to be.*

Thus I became a Machinist. We fled deep into the mountains of the north. I took all the knowledge that I had accumulated over twenty years of being with Hekate, and I used all of it. I was familiar with her tactics; I knew her patterns better than anyone. I knew the loyalties of the people closest to her; I knew many of their secrets. All of these became important tools in our fight.

There were so many things we lost. My eye, a few months after I'd defected. Xiuqing a few months after that, killed in an ambush against Hekate's forces. Shao Weiyi himself died several years after I'd joined: years of stress and the fighting got to him, he didn't have the constitution for it. But me, I lived on like a roach. I continued the fight they had started. I kept the name she had given me, I blatantly used it. Lady Han. I wanted her to know exactly who her opponent was. In me she found a real opponent in her game of xiangqi.

And now? She's dead. I'm still here. The board has been knocked off the table, the pieces scattered everywhere. Have I won? Is this considered a victory? Who knows?

Who knows?

Chapter Eleven

So, does it change anything? Knowing that my fight was driven not by the desire for a greater good but by petty revenge? Do you think it all tainted now? Or does it matter to you? It was a noble cause, wasn't it? We made people's lives better. We gave people hope. Do you care why I did it?

Well, that's it. I've talked enough. Now's your turn. Tell me. What were you here for? What did you have to tell me that was so important to interrupt my grief? What happened with this person who sent you to me, this Chuwan?

Chapter Twelve

I see.

Chapter Thirteen

Sonami, eh? What a turn of events. Oh, what a twist! The fortunes must be having a laugh. *I'm* having a laugh. After all my years of effort, one of her own children was her downfall? I should have seen that coming! I couldn't have seen it coming.

Oh, I remember that child: such a strange, intense personality, even as a sprout. She practically raised the twins, since their mother was so busy, and look how they turned out.

I knew Sonami was running secret experiments in the mountains, but I would never have imagined. To *engineer* a prophet to control the hand of fate—a mad concept to even think of, much less *attempt*. Did she succeed? She must have. She must have. Of course, of *course*! It all makes sense now. That's how the assassin got past all the wards and security surrounding Hekate. That's how it all looked like a coincidence. That's how . . .

It was Sonami. She arranged her mother's death. And now she sits on the throne.

I'm sorry. I'm sorry, I have to laugh. Don't you see how

ironic it is? You know what they say: a crooked founda-
tion leads to a slanted building. It's true. Sonami . . . oh,
she'll be worse than her mother, I'll tell you. She started
off cold. The seventh of Hekate's children, having to vie
with everyone else for Mother's attention? The oldest,
Tamiya, had fifteen years on her, already near an adult
when she was born. Her ambition must have driven her
wild. A quiet child. The dangerous sort of quiet. Just bid-
ing her time, you know?

Trust no one. You never know who will betray you.
Well, Hekate. You died exactly the way you lived.

Akeha will be pleased to know this. And Rider too, obviously. "Pleased" may be the wrong word. But thank you
for this information. Your beloved has not passed in vain.
We know what we have to do now.

Join us? After everything I've told you? Child, it's your
funeral. Why not. Why not? We could use the help of
someone like you.

Sit, for now. You've earned your rest. Let's have another round of wine. Come, now. You've heard my story,
now let me hear yours.

Tell me about the woman you lost.

Acknowledgments

Getting to the fourth book in a series, no matter how short, is an endeavor that takes a lot of effort and induces more than its fair share of tears. It is not an undertaking that can be done alone. To that end I would like to thank my editor, Carl Engle-Laird, for his unending patience and understanding as I worked through the difficult gestations of these books. To my agent, DongWon, for always having my back and knowing what to say. To the incredible team at Tor.com Publishing for their support of the series. But most of all, I give thanks to you, the reader. I would be nothing and no one without you.

About the Author

Author photograph © Nicholas Lee

JY YANG is the author of the Tensorate series, which began with *The Black Tides of Heaven* and *The Red Threads of Fortune*. A finalist for the Hugo, Nebula, and World Fantasy Awards, they are also a lapsed journalist, a former practicing scientist, and a master of hermitry. They are a queer, non-binary, postcolonial, intersectional feminist, and have more than two dozen pieces of short fiction published. They live in Singapore and have an MA in creative writing from the University of East Anglia.

TOR·COM

Science fiction. Fantasy. The universe.

And related subjects.

*

More than just a publisher's website, *Tor.com*
is a venue for **original fiction, comics,** and
discussion of the entire field of SF and fantasy,
in all media and from all sources. Visit our site
today—and join the conversation yourself.